United States Presidents

Woodrow Wilson

Paul Joseph
ABDO Publishing Company

visit us at
www.abdopub.com

Published by ABDO Publishing Company, 4940 Viking Drive, Edina, Minnesota 55435. Copyright © 2001 by Abdo Consulting Group, Inc. International copyrights reserved in all countries. No part of this book may be reproduced in any form without written permission from the publisher.

Printed in the United States.

Photo credits: Archive Photos, Corbis, AP/Wide World Photos

Contributing Editors: Bob Italia and Kate A. Furlong
Book design/maps: Patrick Laurel

Library of Congress Cataloging-in-Publication Data

Joseph, Paul, 1970-
    Woodrow Wilson / by Paul Joseph.
        p.   cm. -- (United States presidents)
    Includes index.
    Summary: Follows the life and career of the scholar and educator who was president of the United States during World War I.
    ISBN 1-56239-812-1
    1. Wilson, Woodrow, 1856-1924--Juvenile literature.
 2. Presidents--United States--Biography--Juvenile literature.
 [1. Wilson, Woodrow, 1856-1924. 2. Presidents.]   I. Title.
 II. Series: United States presidents (Edina, Minn.)
 E767.J78   1998
 973.91'3'092--dc21
    [B]   98-4908
                                                    CIP
                                                     AP

Contents

Woodrow Wilson

*W*oodrow Wilson was the twenty-eighth president of the United States. His honest, fair leadership made him one of America's greatest presidents.

As a student, Wilson studied history and government. After college, he worked as a lawyer and a writer. He was also a college professor.

Wilson's leadership skills soon began to show. He became the president of Princeton University. Then he served as governor of New Jersey. In 1912, he was elected president of the United States.

President Wilson served two terms. During this time, he created many new laws to help Americans. He led the nation through **World War I**. And he wrote a peace plan that earned praise from world leaders.

After Wilson left the White House, he led a quiet life. He spent time with family and friends. Woodrow Wilson died in 1924.

President Woodrow Wilson

Woodrow Wilson (1856-1924)
Twenty-eighth President

BORN:	December 28, 1856
PLACE OF BIRTH:	Staunton, Virginia
ANCESTRY:	Scots-Irish
FATHER:	Joseph Ruggles Wilson (1822-1903)
MOTHER:	Janet "Jessie" Woodrow Wilson (1826-1888)
WIVES:	First wife: Ellen Louise Axson (1860-1914)
	Second wife: Edith Bolling Galt (1872-1961)
CHILDREN:	Margaret, Jessie, Eleanor
EDUCATION:	Private tutors, Davidson College, Princeton University, University of Virginia Law School, Johns Hopkins University
RELIGION:	Presbyterian
OCCUPATION:	Lawyer, historian, professor, president of Princeton University
MILITARY SERVICE:	None

POLITICAL PARTY:	Democrat
OFFICES HELD:	Governor of New Jersey
AGE AT INAUGURATION:	56
YEARS SERVED:	1913-1921
VICE PRESIDENT:	Thomas Marshall
DIED:	February 3, 1924, Washington, D.C., age 67
CAUSE OF DEATH:	Natural causes

Detail Area

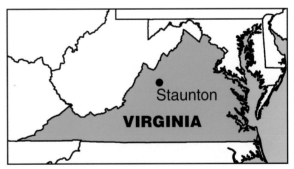

Staunton

VIRGINIA

Birthplace of Woodrow Wilson

Young Tommy

*T*homas Woodrow Wilson was born in Staunton, Virginia, on December 28, 1856. He was called Tommy for most of his young life.

Tommy's mother was Janet Woodrow. She was the daughter of a Presbyterian minister. Tommy's father was Joseph Ruggles Wilson. He, too, was a Presbyterian minister.

Tommy had two older sisters, Annie and Marion. He also had a younger brother, Joseph Jr. When Tommy was a year old, he and his family moved to Augusta, Georgia.

Tommy grew up during the **Civil War**. The war closed most southern schools. So Tommy did not attend classes until he was nine years old.

In school, Tommy had difficulty reading. So his father also taught him at home. He took Tommy to many local shops and factories. Tommy learned to describe everything that he saw. At home, Tommy read the Bible every day. By the time he was 12, his reading problems were over.

Woodrow Wilson's birthplace in Staunton, Virginia

Off to College

*I*n 1873, Wilson attended Davidson College in North Carolina. He studied there for a year and then quit. But he spent the next year reading and studying at home.

Wilson returned to college in 1875. He began classes at the College of New Jersey. It later changed its named to Princeton University. While there, Wilson studied history and government. He also joined a **debate** club. And he worked on the school's newspaper.

In 1879, Wilson graduated from college. Then he began attending the University of Virginia Law School. Soon he grew ill and had to quit. But he

Wilson's 1879 class picture

kept studying at home. In 1882,
Wilson opened his own law office
in Atlanta, Georgia.

The next year, Wilson traveled
to Rome, Georgia, on business.
While there, he met Ellen Louise
Axson. They became friends and
soon fell in love.

Back home, Wilson's law
business was slow. And he found
his cases boring. So Wilson closed
his law office. He decided to get
more education.

Ellen Louise Axson

In 1883, Wilson began classes
at Johns Hopkins University in Baltimore, Maryland. He studied
to be a college professor. In 1885, he wrote his first book,
Congressional Government. It earned him great praise. That same
year, he married Ellen.

Wilson graduated from Johns Hopkins in 1886. Soon after,
he dropped the name Thomas and called himself Woodrow.

Professor

*T*he Wilsons moved to Bryn Mawr, Pennsylvania, in 1886. Wilson took a job at Bryn Mawr College. He taught history and political **economy**.

That year, the Wilsons had a daughter, Margaret. Jessie was born in 1887. And Eleanor followed in 1889. Wilson was a loving father. He liked reading aloud to his family. And he enjoyed playing games with his children.

In 1888, Wilson became a professor at Wesleyan University in Connecticut. Besides teaching, he coached the school football team.

In 1889, Wilson published a textbook on modern governments called *The State*. The next year, he became a law professor at Princeton University.

Wilson had great success at Princeton. He became the school's most popular teacher. And he wrote many articles and books to support his family.

In 1902, Princeton elected Wilson as its president. A few years later, he introduced a new way of teaching. It brought teachers and students together in small classes.

Wilson also tried to reorganize the university into smaller colleges. But the Princeton **alumni** did not approve of Wilson's plan. Still, Wilson's leadership at Princeton made him famous.

In 1909, Wilson had problems with the **dean** of the Graduate School. They disagreed on the location of a new graduate college. The fight ended when the dean gained power over the project. It was a bitter loss for Wilson. He began thinking about a new career.

Woodrow Wilson (circled) with the professors from Wesleyan University in 1889

Governor

*B*ecause of Wilson's success at Princeton, his friends urged him to go into politics. They helped him get the support of James Smith Jr. Smith was an important member of the **Democratic** party in New Jersey. He agreed to **nominate** Wilson for governor.

Wilson agreed to the nomination. But he would not allow other Democrats to interfere with his plans. In 1910, Wilson won the election.

Wilson worked hard for government **reforms**. He formed a public service **commission**. It controlled the prices and services of **public utilities** and railroads. He formed an **insurance** system to help injured workers. He passed new election laws. And he fought for school reforms.

Governor Wilson's success earned him more national attention. In 1912, the Democrats chose him as their presidential candidate. Indiana governor Thomas R. Marshall became Wilson's vice president.

The **Republican** party renominated President William Howard Taft. Former president Theodore Roosevelt ran for the **Progressive** party.

Wilson **campaigned** hard with his "New Freedom" program. He promised to reduce **tariffs**, strengthen **antitrust** laws, and reorganize the country's banking system. Voters liked Wilson's ideas. They elected him president.

Wilson makes a speech during the 1912 presidential campaign.

The Making of the Twenty-eighth United States President

1856
Born December 28 in Staunton, Virginia

1857
Family moves to Augusta, Georgia

1865
Enters school

1873
Enters Davidson College

1885
Marries Ellen Axson; writes *Congressional Government*

1886
Graduates from Johns Hopkins University; teaches at Bryn Mawr College

1888
Professor of history at Wesleyan University

1889
Writes *The State*

1912
Elected president of the United States

1913
Underwood Tariff Act; Federal Reserve Act; income tax approved

1914
World War I begins; Ellen Axson Wilson dies August 6; Federal Trade Commission; Clayton Antitrust Act

1915
Marries Edith Bolling Galt December 18

1916
Re-elected president

PRESIDENTIAL

Woodrow Wilson

"There must be, not a balance of power, but a community of power; not organized rivalries, but an organized common peace."

1875
Enters Princeton University

1879
Graduates from Princeton; enters University of Virginia Law School

1882
Starts law firm in Atlanta, Georgia

Historic Events during Wilson's Presidency

- Henry Ford invents the assembly line
- Panama Canal opened
- First transcontinental telephone call
- Russian Revolution

1890
Professor of law at Princeton

1902
Elected president of Princeton

1910
Elected governor of New Jersey

1917
U.S. declares war on Germany

1918
World War I ends

1919
Treaty of Versailles signed; League of Nations formed; Prohibition begins; Wilson suffers stroke

1920
Women's Suffrage; receives the Nobel Peace Prize; does not run for re-election

1924
Dies on February 3

YEARS

President Wilson

Woodrow Wilson took office on March 4, 1913. He wanted to keep his **campaign** promises. So he quickly began working with **Congress** to pass new laws.

Congress passed the Underwood **Tariff** Act. It reduced tariffs and made goods cheaper for Americans. But reducing tariffs meant the government had less money. So Congress approved the Sixteenth **Amendment**. It made Americans pay an income tax.

Congress passed Wilson's other laws, too. The Federal Reserve Act of 1913 created 12 new banks for the government. It also created a new

Woodrow Wilson is sworn in as president on March 4, 1913.

American **currency**. In 1914, the Federal Trade **Commission** Act outlawed unfair business practices. And the Clayton **Antitrust** Act made **labor unions** legal.

While Wilson worked with **Congress**, **World War I** started in Europe in July 1914. Wilson promised to keep America out of the war.

Edith Bolling Galt

That same year, Wilson suffered a personal loss. His wife died in August. Wilson was sad and lonely. He had trouble working.

In 1915, Germany sunk a passenger ship called the *Lusitania*. It killed innocent British and American passengers. Americans were angry. But Wilson stayed calm. He convinced Germany to stop attacking passenger and merchant ships.

Later that year, Wilson's personal life grew brighter. He married his friend Edith Bolling Galt.

The year 1916 was an election year. Voters liked Wilson's new laws. And they were glad he had kept America out of World War I. He was re-elected to a second term.

The Seven "Hats" of the U.S. President

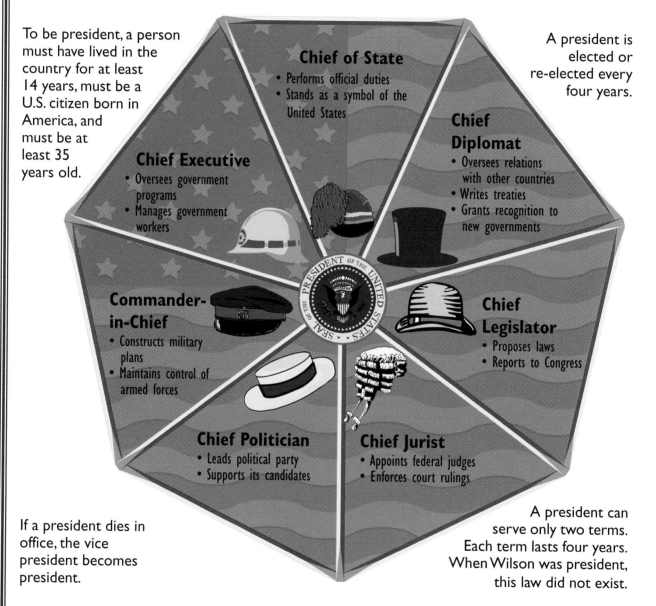

To be president, a person must have lived in the country for at least 14 years, must be a U.S. citizen born in America, and must be at least 35 years old.

A president is elected or re-elected every four years.

Chief of State
- Performs official duties
- Stands as a symbol of the United States

Chief Diplomat
- Oversees relations with other countries
- Writes treaties
- Grants recognition to new governments

Chief Executive
- Oversees government programs
- Manages government workers

Commander-in-Chief
- Constructs military plans
- Maintains control of armed forces

Chief Legislator
- Proposes laws
- Reports to Congress

Chief Politician
- Leads political party
- Supports its candidates

Chief Jurist
- Appoints federal judges
- Enforces court rulings

If a president dies in office, the vice president becomes president.

A president can serve only two terms. Each term lasts four years. When Wilson was president, this law did not exist.

As president, Woodrow Wilson had seven jobs.

The Three Branches of the U.S. Government

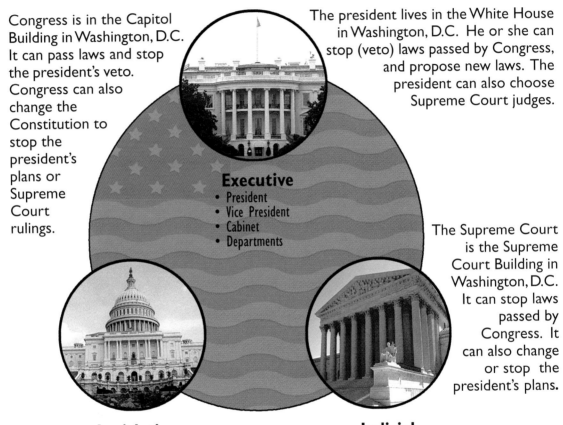

Congress is in the Capitol Building in Washington, D.C. It can pass laws and stop the president's veto. Congress can also change the Constitution to stop the president's plans or Supreme Court rulings.

The president lives in the White House in Washington, D.C. He or she can stop (veto) laws passed by Congress, and propose new laws. The president can also choose Supreme Court judges.

Executive
- President
- Vice President
- Cabinet
- Departments

The Supreme Court is the Supreme Court Building in Washington, D.C. It can stop laws passed by Congress. It can also change or stop the president's plans.

Legislative (Congress)
- Senate
- House of Representatives

Judicial
- Supreme Court
- Federal courts

The U.S. Constitution formed three government branches. Each branch has power over the others. So no single group or person can control the country. The Constitution calls this "separation of powers."

World War I

*W*ilson tried to help European leaders end the war. But Germany broke its promise not to attack passenger and merchant ships. And the British uncovered a secret German plan. It said if Germany won the war, it would give some of America's land to Mexico.

Germany's actions angered Americans. Wilson realized he had no choice but to enter the war. On April 2, 1917, he asked **Congress** to declare war on Germany. Four days later, Congress approved and the U.S. entered **World War I**.

Wilson traveled around the country speaking about the war. In January 1918, he gave a speech called Fourteen Points. It was a peace plan. An important part of the plan was a League of Nations. The league would carry out the peace plan and prevent future wars.

In the following months, Germany's military lost major battles. German leaders sent Wilson a message. They accepted his Fourteen Points. On November 11, 1918, Germany signed an agreement to stop fighting. This is called Armistice Day.

After Armistice Day, Wilson traveled to France. He attended the Paris Peace Conference. It was a meeting of world leaders. They signed the Versailles Treaty on June 28, 1919. It officially ended **World War I**. And it stated the peace plan for Europe after the war.

Leaders of the Paris Peace Conference (left to right): Vittorio Orlando of Italy, Lloyd George of Great Britain, Georges Clemenceaus of France, and Woodrow Wilson of the United States.

The Versailles Treaty did not include all of Wilson's Fourteen Points. But he made sure it included the League of Nations. Wilson returned to the U.S. with the Versailles Treaty. He had to get the U.S. **Senate** to approve it.

Many Americans disliked the League of Nations. They did not want America involved in Europe's problems. They also felt it weakened America's power. So Wilson traveled around the nation in 1919. He tried to convince Americans that the League of Nations was a good idea.

When Wilson returned to Washington, D.C., he had a stroke. It **paralyzed** him. He was too weak to fight the Senate. The Senate voted against the Versailles Treaty because of its League of Nations.

As Wilson recovered, **Congress** passed two **Amendments** to the **Constitution**. The Eighteenth Amendment passed in 1919. It made buying and selling alcohol illegal. This is called Prohibition. The Nineteenth Amendment passed in 1920. It gave women the right to vote. This is called Women's Suffrage.

The year 1920 also brought another election. Wilson did not run. **Republican** Warren G. Harding won the election.

Later that year, Wilson received the **Nobel Peace Prize** for his work on the League of Nations. He retired from the White House in 1921.

These women from Stillwater, Minnesota, were the first to vote under the Nineteenth Amendment.

Wilson Retires

Wilson lived a quiet life in Washington, D.C. He regained some use of his arms and legs. And he formed a law partnership. But he was too weak to work.

At times, Wilson went to the movies or saw plays. He also liked to listen to books and magazines read aloud to him. Sometimes, he invited friends over for lunch.

Wilson never gave up hope that America would join the League of Nations. He believed he was right about the League and the peace terms of **World War I**.

On February 3, 1924, Wilson died in his sleep. Two days later, he was buried in Washington Cathedral. He is the only president buried in Washington, D.C.

Many historians call Woodrow Wilson one of the greatest U.S. presidents. He worked well with **Congress**, passing many laws and **reforms**. He also led America through a troubled time in world history. And he helped end World War I.

Wilson's greatest accomplishment was the League of Nations. It led to the creation of today's **United Nations**.

Wilson's house on S Street in Washington, D.C.

Fast Facts

- Woodrow Wilson is the only U.S. president to have a Ph.D.

- President Wilson kept a flock of sheep on the White House lawn to help raise wool for the war effort.

- President Wilson is one of six presidents to have changed his first name.

- President Wilson established the national observance of Mother's Day.

- Wilson was the first president to cross the Atlantic Ocean while in office. He traveled to the Paris Peace Conference on a ship called the *George Washington*.

- Wilson was the first president to live in Washington, D.C., during retirement.

President Wilson boards the **George Washington.**

Glossary

alumni - graduates of a college or university.

Amendment - a change to the Constitution of the United States.

antitrust - regulations against businesses that hurt free trade or interfere with competition.

campaign - an organized series of events with the goal of electing a person to public office.

Civil War - a war between groups within the same country. The Union and the Confederate States of America fought from 1861 to 1865.

commission - a group of people chosen to perform certain duties.

Congress - the lawmaking body of the U.S. It is made up of the Senate and the House of Representatives. It meets in Washington, D.C.

Constitution - the laws that govern the United States.

currency - the money used in a country.

dean - a person at a university who is in charge of discipline, activities, studies, and guidance of students.

debate - to discuss a question or topic.

Democrat - a person who is liberal and believes in a large government.

economy - the way a state or nation uses its money, goods, and natural resources.

insurance - a contract that helps people pay their bills if they are sick or hurt. People with insurance pay money each month to keep the contract.

labor union - a group formed to help workers receive their rights.

Nobel Peace Prize - a prize given each year to a person who works hard for world peace.

nominate - to name a person as a candidate for office.

paralyzed - when a person cannot move his or her arms or legs.

Progressive - a political party that split from the Republican party around 1912. Also known as the Bull Moose party.

public utility - a company that provides an important service, such as supplying gas, water, or electricity.

reform - to make a change for the better.

Republican - a person who is conservative and believes in small government.

Senate - the upper house in the U.S. Congress. Citizens elect senators to make laws for the nation.

tariff - fees or taxes placed on goods from foreign countries.

United Nations - a worldwide group formed in 1945 to promote peace.

World War I - 1914 to 1918, fought in Europe. The United States, Great Britain, France, Russia, and their allies were on one side. Germany, Austria-Hungary, and their allies were on the other side. The war began when Archduke Ferdinand of Austria was assassinated. America joined the war in 1917 because Germany began attacking ships that weren't involved in the war.

Internet Sites

The Presidents of the United States of America
http://www.whitehouse.gov/WH/glimpse/presidents/html/presidents.html
Part of the White House Web site.

Woodrow Wilson House
http://www.woodrowwilsonhouse.org
This site is dedicated to preserving the home and works of Woodrow Wilson.

These sites are subject to change. Go to your favorite search engine and type in United States Presidents for more sites.

Index